Mallory Makes a Difference

For Becca and Adam. Always!
And for all my readers. Thanks for loving
Mallory as much as I do.
—L.B.F.

For Juliette, who will soon be reading
these books, may they be an inspiration
to you always.
—J.K.

Mallory Makes a Difference

Project Notebook

by Laurie Friedman

illustrations by Jennifer Kalis

darbycreek

MINNEAPOLIS

CONTENTS

A WORD FROM MALLORY

My name is Mallory McDonald, like the restaurant, but no relation. I have a cat named Cheeseburger and a brother named Max. I'm in fifth grade, and I'm so excited because my favorite time of year is finally here.

It's fall, which means all of the best holidays are right around the corner!

First up is Halloween. I love dressing up, getting candy, and having fun with my friends. Then it's Thanksgiving. There's nothing yummier than feasting with my family. And Christmas is the most fun of all. I love putting up the tree, baking cookies, going caroling and, of course, exchanging gifts.

My only problem now is deciding how I'm going to celebrate Halloween.

Half of my friends are going to a party at Mary Ann's house, where they'll eat pizza and watch a scary movie. The other half are meeting up at Pamela's to go trick-or-treating.

I know I can't be two places at once, but I don't want to miss out on the party or going trick-or-treating. For the last week, I've been trying to decide what I would rather do.

I made a pros and cons list. I tried flipping a coin. I even tried writing the words *party* and *trick-or-treating* on note cards and told my cat, Cheeseburger, to point her paw to the place she thought I should go. But I still couldn't decide.

Tonight, though, I realized something important —I don't have to pick one place. I can go both places. So on Halloween, I'm going to go to Mary Ann's house first, have pizza, and then skip the movie and go to Pamela's to trick-or-treat.

Problem solved!

Happy Halloween!

(UN)HAPPY
HALLOWEEN

"Dad, let's go!" I try not to pace in the family room while I wait for Dad. But it's hard not to. It's Halloween, which means I have two places to be and no time to waste.

When Dad and I are finally in the van on the way to Mary Ann's house, I go over the schedule with him again.

"I'll call you when we're done eating pizza. Then you're going to pick me up

from Mary Ann's and take me to Pamela's house so I can trick-or-treat."

Dad glances at me. "Are you sure you don't want to just stay at Mary Ann's?"

I let out a breath. Mom and Dad think that I'm trying to do too much in one night and that I should have picked either Mary Ann's party or trick-or-treating. But I really want to do both things. "Dad, please. We've already talked about this."

"Aye, aye, Captain," says Dad with a wink. He and Mom are wearing matching pirate costumes to give out candy to trick-or-treaters. I know he thinks his pirate imitation is funny, but this is no laughing matter.

"Dad, when you pick me up, please don't forget to bring my Halloween costume so I can change in the van on the way to Pamela's house," I say as we pull up in front of Mary Ann's house.

"Be off with you, matey," Dad says in his pirate voice. "I know what to do."

I give Dad a smile as I get out of the van. "Thanks," I say.

As I walk up to Mary Ann's front door, I think about who is coming to her party. Zoe, Arielle, Danielle, Hannah, and Grace will all be here. Chloe Jennifer, April, Emma, Dawn, and Brittany are going to

Pamela's. I really wish everyone could have done one thing together, but that isn't the case.

When I ring the bell, Joey opens the door. "Happy Halloween!" he says.

He's wearing vampire fangs that make his voice sound funny when he speaks. I can't help but laugh. "Great costume," I say.

"Thanks," Joey says, smiling. "I'm leaving to go trick-or-treating with Pete and Devon," he adds. "The girls are in Mary Ann's room if you want to go up."

"Have fun!" I say.

When I walk into Mary Ann's room, Zoe, Arielle, and Danielle are already there.

"Mallory!" says Mary Ann like she's glad I came. She knows that I was torn about what I wanted to do and that I'm planning to leave after we eat. "We're just waiting for Hannah and Grace to get here before we order the pizza."

"Cool," I say and look at the clock on my phone. I just hope they get here soon. I'm supposed to be at Pamela's house in an hour to start trick-or-treating.

"Do you want to paint your nails?" asks Danielle.

"We brought black and orange polish," says Arielle.

"Sure." I plop down on the floor next to Zoe, who is already painting her nails in Halloween colors.

"Look," says Zoe when she's done. She wiggles her fingers. She painted her nails orange with black spots and stripes. "Cute, huh?"

"Your nails look like baby leopards," says Mary Ann. She giggles.

I decide to paint all my nails orange except for my pointer fingers. I paint those nails black. By the time I'm done, Hannah and Grace arrive.

"I'm going to ask my mom to order the pizza now," says Mary Ann. "Who wants pepperoni, and who wants plain cheese?" she asks.

She counts up who wants what and then writes it down on a notepad. I hope the pizza will get here fast. I have to leave in forty-five minutes.

While we wait for the pizza, we hang out in the kitchen, talking and eating chips

and dip. "What's your favorite kind of Halloween candy?" asks Hannah.

"I like lollipops," says Grace.

"I like anything chocolate," says Arielle.

"Mmm, me too," says Danielle.

Halloween candy seems like a weird thing to be talking about, especially since no one who came to the party wanted to go trick-or-treating. I try to focus on what everyone is saying, but it's hard not to look at the time on my phone.

All of my friends at Pamela's are going to start trick-or-treating in twenty minutes, and there's still no sign of the pizza. I decide to go into the bathroom and text Pamela.

I wait ten minutes and then another ten minutes but still no sign of the pizza.

I don't know if I should stay or go. If I go, I don't get to eat pizza. And if I stay, I can't trick-or-treat.

I do an *eenie, meenie, miney, mo* in my head, but it doesn't help. I feel my phone buzzing. I pull it out of my pocket and read the text from Pamela.

I walk out of the kitchen and text her back.

Pamela

Still at Mary Ann's.

Waiting for pizza to get here

Hurry!

Tell that to the pizza guy.

ha-ha!

I'll do my best!

But it's not OK. I'm hungry and I'm late. This is NOT how I planned Halloween.

I text Dad to come and get me. Maybe by the time he gets here, the pizza will have already arrived and I will have eaten it.

As I put my phone back into my pocket, Mary Ann's mom comes into the kitchen. "Girls, I'm so sorry the pizza is taking so long," she says. "I just called and the restaurant said Halloween is a busy night, but they promised the pizza is on its way."

Unfortunately for me, Dad is a faster driver than the delivery guy.

What's faster than a speeding bullet? | What's slower than a snail?

"I guess I have to go," I say when I hear him honk his horn.

Mary Ann frowns. "You don't want to stay for pizza?" she asks.

Actually, I do. I'm starving, but Dad is here. I say bye and race out to the van. When I get inside, Dad hands me my witch costume. "How was the pizza?" he asks.

I know if I explain what happened, he'll say I need to eat dinner, especially before I eat a bunch of candy. But I also don't want

to lie. "Tell you about it later," I say. "I have
to get dressed and text Pamela to find out
where everyone's trick-or-treating."

Dad opens his mouth, and then he
closes it. I'm not sure what he was going
to say, but I'm relieved when he doesn't
say anything.

I slip on my costume and then buckle my
seat belt as Dad pulls out of the driveway. I
pull out my phone and text Pamela.

"Mallory, where are your friends?" Dad

asks as we get closer
to Pamela's house.

I stare down at
my phone. "Pamela
hasn't answered yet,"
I mumble.

Dad looks at me
like he gets what's
going on and feels

sorry for me. "Why don't I drive around the neighborhood? I bet we can find your friends."

"Sure," I say. There's a lump in my throat. I feel like something is stuck, and it's obviously not Halloween candy. As we drive from street to street, I text Pamela again to try and find out where they are. But she still doesn't answer.

When I finally spot my friends, Dad pulls over and I hop out of the van.

"Mallory!" says Dawn. "What took you so long?"

"Look at how much candy we've gotten," says Brittany. She opens up the pillowcase she's carrying so that I can see how much candy is in it.

"I'm sorry I didn't text you back," Pamela says. "I didn't hear my phone."

"We're going to do a few more houses,

and then we're going back to Pamela's house to trade candy," says April.

"We'll share what we got with you," says Chloe Jennifer. I can tell they've had enough trick-or-treating, but they feel bad that I haven't had any.

"Don't worry," I say. I wave to Dad like everything is fine and he can go. But as he drives off, part of me wants to just get in the van and go home with him.

I've had enough Halloween for one night.

IN THE NEWS

"Why the long face?" asks Mom when I walk into the kitchen. "Are you feeling OK?"

"I'm fine," I say. But the truth is that I'm in a grumpy mood.

I pour cereal into a bowl and top it with sliced bananas and milk. Then I sit down at the table and eat a spoonful. I see Mom and Dad look at each other. I was quiet the whole car ride home when Dad picked me up from Pamela's. Then

I went straight to bed. I know my parents can tell something is wrong.

Ever since I woke up, I've been thinking about last night. No pizza. Not much candy. And not much fun.

Halloween definitely didn't turn out the way I planned.

Dad puts down the newspaper and looks at me. "Anything you'd like to talk about?" he asks.

I put my spoon down. I tell Mom and Dad about missing the pizza at Mary Ann's house and then missing most of the trick-or-treating.

I wait for Mom and Dad to say something like *You shouldn't have tried to do two things,* or *We tried to warn you.*

But my parents surprise me. "I'm sorry your night didn't work out the way you wanted," says Mom.

Dad takes a sip of his coffee. "The good news is that Halloween was just one holiday and there are several more coming up. Hopefully, Thanksgiving and Christmas will be better."

Mom smiles at me. "Maybe there's something you can do to make them extra special," she says.

"I'd like them to be better," I tell my parents. I pick up my spoon and take another bite of cereal. The truth is that I don't think they could be much worse. As I eat my cereal, Max walks into the kitchen and sticks a slice of bread in the toaster.

"Would you like some eggs?" Mom asks Max.

"No thanks," says my brother. "I'm not that hungry. I ate too much candy last night." As he waits for his bread to toast, he gives a bite of scrambled eggs to Champ

and talks about the party he went to.

It sounds like fun and I'm glad he had a good time, but it doesn't make me feel any better about the night I had. I should have listened to Mom and Dad when they tried to tell me I was doing too much.

Max sits down with his toast and starts eating.

Dad takes a sip of coffee and turns the page of the newspaper. "Here's a cool story," he says. He reads an article aloud. It's about a group of high school juniors who hosted weekly bake sales to raise money to host a Halloween party for underprivileged kids.

"Over one hundred kids attended the party," says Dad. He reads a quote from a little boy who went to the party.

"They gave everyone candy and

Fern Falls High Juniors Host Halloween Bash.

costumes. There was a DJ, and we played scary games. I had so much fun. It was the best Halloween ever!"

"My history teacher told us about that party," says Max. "When she heard the kids at the high school organized it, she said that next year she's going to try to do the same thing at the middle school."

"That's a good idea," says Mom.

"Here's a quote from one of the girls

who organized the party," says Dad.

"'Seeing all the happy faces of the kids at the party made it the best Halloween ever,' says Jenny Perez, a junior at Fern Falls High School."

Mom looks over Dad's shoulder at the newspaper. "It sounds like a great night for the kids who attended the party and for the kids who organized it," she says. "I think it's wonderful that the kids who organized the party made a difference in the lives of other people."

I finish my cereal and then take my bowl to the sink. While I rinse it out, I think about what Jenny Perez said. Seeing all the happy faces of the kids who came to the party made it the best Halloween she's ever had.

As I sling my backpack over my shoulder, I can't help but think about the difference between Jenny and me.

I thought I had the worst Halloween ever.

She thought she had the best
Halloween ever.

When it comes to holiday planning,
maybe I, Mallory McDonald, can learn
something from her.

Who would you rather be?

AN IDEA

"It's your turn," says Max.

I point to the chart on our bathroom wall. "I cleaned the bathroom last time. It's your turn." Our chore chart speaks the truth, and Max knows it.

His shoulders sag. "I have a math test tomorrow," he says.

"Tomorrow is Sunday," I remind my brother.

"Yeah, right," says Max like he was confused. "I meant Monday."

But I don't think my brother mixed up his days. I just think he doesn't want to clean the bathroom. I start to walk back to my room, but Max stops me.

"Please!" he says. "If you'll clean it this time, I'll do it the next three times."

I might be younger than Max, but I'm not stupid. I know his tricks. "You know you won't," I say.

Max goes into his room. He comes back with a notebook and pen. "I'll even put it in writing." Max has never done that before. I accept his offer.

> I, Max McDonald, promise to clean the bathroom three (3) times.
>
> Max McDonald

As I scrub the tub, I think about Halloween. It was a week ago, but the article Dad read about the students at the high school who held the Halloween party for underprivileged kids is stuck in my brain.

What they did is really nice and really cool.

When I finish cleaning the bathtub, I spray glass cleaner on the mirror and start wiping it off with a rag.

I can't change what happened on Halloween, but I remember what Mom said about Thanksgiving. It's coming up, and maybe there's something I can do to make it extra special. I'd like to do something like the high school kids did. It would be nice to help other people have a great holiday.

The only question is, *What could I do?*

When I finish cleaning the bathroom, I sit down at my desk with Cheeseburger to try and answer that question.

I scribble down a few ideas. But none of them seem right.

I need someone who can help me think—and I know just the right person.

I change into my pajamas, slip my feet into my fuzzy duck slippers, and walk upstairs to Mom and Dad's room. Mom is in bed reading a book.

"Can I come in?" I ask.

Mom puts her book down and pats the empty spot next to her. I plop down on the bed beside Mom and tell her what's on my mind.

"For Thanksgiving, I'd like to do something that helps other people. But I don't know what that something should be."

Mom smiles at me like she likes the way I'm thinking. "You must have some ideas," Mom says.

"I was thinking that we could have a party at my school and do what the high school kids did." I pause. "But that doesn't seem very Thanksgiving-y."

"Hmmm," says Mom. "Any other ideas?"

"I thought about doing something to improve the school, like planting flowers. But that doesn't seem quite right either." I talk faster. "Since it's Thanksgiving, it could be nice to do something with food."

"You know, there are lots of people in Fern Falls who don't have enough food to eat," says Mom. "Not just on Thanksgiving but on a daily basis."

I think about that for a minute. "What if I organize a food drive at school? Students could bring in canned goods to help families in need. That way, those families could have food so they can enjoy the holiday."

"That's a great idea!" Mom says.

As I think about doing a food drive, all kinds of ideas start rolling around in my brain. "It could be a contest," I say. "There could be a prize for the grade that brings in the most cans."

"That could work," says Mom.

"It could be a really good prize so that kids bring in a lot of cans. I think there should be no school for a week for the class that wins," I say.

Mom laughs. "That might be a bit much. First, you need to talk to Mrs. Finney about

having a food drive.
As the principal,
she'd have to
approve it before
you get started."

The
Lady
in
charge

Mrs. Finney
Fern Falls
PRINCIPAL

"Thanks!" I hop
off her bed. "I
have to go. I have
a phone call to
make," I say over
my shoulder.

"Wait!" says Mom. "It's the weekend. You
can't call Mrs. Finney. You'll have to wait
and talk to her at school on Monday."

Now it's my turn to laugh. "I wasn't
going to call Mrs. Finney," I say.

There's someone else I need to talk to.

AN UNEXPECTED PARTNER

Last night after I talked to Mom, I went straight to my room and called Mary Ann. I told her I had an amazing idea that I was sure she would LOVE!

She wanted to know what it was, but I told her my idea was so amazing that I wanted to explain it to her in person. So we made plans to get together tomorrow.

I tossed and turned all night waiting for today to get here. Now, Mom is driving me to Mary Ann's house. As soon as I get there, I'm going to tell Mary Ann my idea for the food drive, and I'm sure she's going to want to do it with me.

Mom drops me off at the Winstons', and I ring their doorbell. It's hard to be patient while I wait for Mary Ann to answer. I thought about asking Mary Ann *and* Chloe Jennifer to help me with my plan. But Chloe Jennifer has a piano recital the weekend before

Thanksgiving and is spending all her spare time practicing.

Mary Ann is the perfect person for the job.

"Hey!" says Mary Ann when she opens the door. "Winnie and Joey and I are watching a great movie. You can watch it with us," she says as she leads the way to their family room.

I don't want to watch a movie. I want to tell Mary Ann about my idea. "Can we talk first?" I ask. I remind her that I have an idea I wanted to tell her about.

"We'll talk when the movie is over," says Mary Ann.

That's not really what I want to do, but it's not like I have a choice. I sit down on the couch between Joey and Mary Ann. "Hi," I say to Joey.

"Shh!" says Winnie.

I try to focus on the movie.

The kids on the TV are pretty excited.
They've just found some important, secret
documents in their grandmother's attic.
I'll be excited when they do whatever it is
they're planning to do with them and the
movie is over.

"Is this the end?" I ask.

"Shh!" Winnie says again.

The kids on TV deliver the documents to
the police, who let their grandmother out
of jail. They reunite and everyone is happy.

Especially me. The movie is finally over!

"Now, are you ready to hear my idea?" I ask Mary Ann as soon as Winnie turns the TV off.

"Sure," says Mary Ann.

All of a sudden, I feel nervous like I did when Devon and I had to present our book report to our class. I want to do a good job explaining this.

I take a deep breath and tell Mary Ann about my plan for organizing a food drive at school. "First, we'd have to talk to Mrs. Finney at school on Monday and get permission to do it. But I'm sure she's going to say yes. I think it's a really good idea. It will help other people, and it will be a lot of fun to do it."

I pause and look at Mary Ann. "But it will be even more fun if we do it together."

I stop talking. It's Mary Ann's turn to say what an amazing idea I have and that she'd love to do it with me, but that's not what she says.

Mary Ann twirls a curl around her finger. "I don't think I want to do it," she says.

I can't believe what I'm hearing. "Why?"
I ask.

Mary Ann shrugs.

But that's not an answer to my question.
I ask again. "Why don't you want to do it?"

Mary Ann lets out a breath. "It just
doesn't sound like fun to me."

"It's not the same kind of fun you
have at a sleepover or when you go to a
swimming pool," I explain. "But it'll be fun
to do a project that helps other people."

Apparently, Mary Ann doesn't feel the same way I do. "I'm just not into it. Sorry," she says. I know that means she's done talking about it.

"Sure," I say like it's not a big deal, but it is to me. I think it's such a good idea, and I'm shocked she can't see that.

"Do you want to hang out in my room?" Mary Ann asks.

We go to Mary Ann's room and play games on her computer. But I have a hard time focusing. I can't believe she didn't want to do the food drive with me.

I can't decide if it's because she doesn't want to do something nice for other people or because she doesn't want to do something with me.

And I'm not sure which of those things bothers me more.

When Mary Ann puts on headphones to

listen to a song, I think about how much
our friendship has changed. In the past,
Mary Ann would have been just as excited
as I am to do this. Lately, I feel like Mary
Ann is a lot more interested in what she
wants to do than in what matters to other
people. I think it's why we're not as close as
we used to be.

When Mom comes to pick me up, I
tell Mary Ann bye and walk down the
stairs. I'm just about to leave when Joey

stops me. "The food drive sounds cool," he says.

"Thanks," I tell him. "I think so too."

Joey hesitates like he's about to say something but isn't sure how to say it. I think I know what he was going to say. "Were you going to tell me not to be upset about Mary Ann not wanting to do the food drive with me?" I ask.

Joey laughs. "Nope," he says. "I was going to ask you if I could do it with you." He grins at me. "Partners?"

"Are you kidding?" My grin is even bigger than Joey's. I can't believe I didn't think to ask him if he wanted to do this with me. I'm so glad he wants to. "Partners!" I say back.

Joey and I high-five. Deciding to work together is only our first step. Now we've got a food drive to plan.

The good news is that she does! "I think it's a wonderful idea for the school to do a food drive," says Mrs. Finney. "I'll contact the Fern Falls Food Bank and coordinate it with them." Then she pauses. "But I'm not sure about the homework-free week."

"Please!" Joey and I say at the same time.

"It will motivate kids to get involved," I explain.

"Since this is the first time we've done this at Fern Falls Elementary, we think it's important to offer something that gets students excited," adds Joey.

Mrs. Finney smiles at us. "You're both very convincing," she says. "We'll do it."

Joey and I look at each other and grin. "I hope our grade wins," he says.

Mrs. Finney laughs. "I think the food drive is a lovely idea, and I'm proud of both of you for thinking of it." Then she gets a serious

READY, SET, GO!

When Joey and I get to school, we meet outside Mrs. Finney's office.

Even though we didn't do anything wrong, walking into the principal's office is kind of scary. "Ready?" asks Joey when Mrs. Finney's secretary, Mr. Price, says she's available to see us.

I nod. I'm wearing my best shirt and skirt so that I make a good impression. And Joey and I talked on the phone last night and rehearsed exactly what we're going to say.

"What can I do for you?" asks Mrs. Finney when we sit down in her office.

I clear my throat and begin. "Joey and I have an idea." I sit up straight in the chair as I talk to Mrs. Finney about the food drive. "We'd like to get kids to bring in canned goods so families in Fern Falls will have what they need for Thanksgiving."

Joey picks up where I leave off. "We were thinking that we could form a committee with two representatives from each grade who would be in charge of getting the kids in their grade to bring in cans."

He explains that we'd like to award a prize to the grade that brings in the most cans. "Maybe you could give a homework-free week to the grade that wins," he says.

When Joey finishes talking, we both look at Mrs. Finney. She's quiet like she's thinking about what we said. It's hard to tell how she feels about our idea.

I cross my toes inside my shoes. I really hope she likes it.

look on her face. "But Thanksgiving is right around the corner. This is going to take a lot of work. Are you up for it?" she asks.

I nod that I am, and Joey does too.

"OK," says Mrs. Finney. "I'm going to assign Mrs. Daily to be your adviser. She'll help you with all the plans."

Even though we're sitting in the principal's office, Joey and I high-five each other. Mrs. Daily was our third-grade teacher, and we both love her.

"It will be awesome to have Mrs. Daily as our adviser," I tell Mrs. Finney.

"I'm glad you're both pleased," she says. "I'll talk to Mrs. Daily this morning. I'm also going to hold an all-school assembly on Wednesday to announce the food drive. I don't think you should talk about this with your friends until they hear about it at the assembly. Since it's a contest, everyone should start collecting cans at the same time."

She pauses and looks at us. "We'll choose reps on Thursday, and you can meet with them Friday to explain what they'll need to do. Students can bring in cans all next week. We'll have an assembly before Thanksgiving to announce the winning class."

"That sounds great," I say.

"Thank you," says Joey.

Mrs. Finney smiles again. "My pleasure. Just let me know if you need anything else."

As Joey and I leave Mrs. Finney's office, we're both super excited about the food drive, and we stay that way all week. On Tuesday, we eat lunch with Mrs. Daily in her classroom so we can start planning what we need to do.

She's just as enthusiastic about the
food drive as we are. "I like that Fern
Falls Elementary is getting involved in
the community in such a helpful way,"
she tells us.

That afternoon, Joey comes to my house
after school. We use the computer in the
kitchen to make sign-up sheets for kids
who want to be grade reps. Then we draw
a poster to announce the food drive.

"I can't wait until tomorrow," says Joey as we color the poster.

I feel the same way.

When I wake up on Wednesday morning, I set a record for getting dressed and eating my breakfast faster than ever. I can hardly wait for the assembly to start.

BE PART OF THE FIRST-EVER FERN FALLS ELEMENTARY FOOD DRIVE. THE GRADE THAT BRINGS IN THE MOST CANS WINS ONE HOMEWORK-FREE WEEK!!! DON'T FORGET YOUR CANS!

As I walk into the auditorium with my friends, everyone is talking about it.

"I wonder what this is about," says Chloe Jennifer.

"I hope it's something good," says Devon.

"Maybe we get extra days off for Thanksgiving," says April.

"I doubt that," says Zoe.

I sit down beside Joey, and Pamela takes the empty seat next to me. Mary Ann sits down in the chair next to Pamela. "What do you think's going on?" I hear her ask.

I can't wait for everyone to find out.

When Mrs. Finney starts the assembly, Joey and I exchange a look.

"Students, I have a special announcement to make," says Mrs. Finney. She tells everyone about the food drive and how it will work.

"Two fifth graders, Mallory McDonald and Joey Winston, came to me with the idea. I thought it was a good one, and that's why we're doing it."

When she says that, everyone who is sitting near Joey and me turns around to look at us. I can feel my face turning red. I'm a little embarrassed but in a good way.

I'm kind of surprised when Mary Ann
leans across Pamela and gives me an
I-can't-believe-you're-doing-this-without-me look.
But all I can do is shrug. I tried to get her to
do it with me, and she didn't want to.

"There will be two class reps from each
grade," says Mrs. Finney. "Sign-up sheets
are outside the gym. If more than two

people from each grade sign up, we will do a random drawing to see who gets the job."

Mrs. Finney continues to explain how the food drive will work. "This is a great opportunity to give back to the community," she says. "It's also an opportunity at school. The grade that brings in the most cans wins a homework-free week."

When she says that, every kid in the auditorium goes crazy.

"Students, your attention, please," Mrs. Finney says from her podium. "I know you're all excited about the idea of a homework-free week, but let's remember we're doing the food drive to help other people, and that's what's most important."

When she finishes talking, she dismisses everyone to go back to class.

As we leave the auditorium, kids crowd around Joey and me. I feel like a movie star.

"What a great idea!" says Chloe Jennifer.

"I'm definitely signing up to be a class rep," says Arielle.

"Me too," says Danielle. "I want to make sure the fifth grade wins."

Everyone is excited about the food drive. Some sixth graders come up to Joey and me and tell us they like the idea and want to get involved. Even first graders are excited. One first-grade boy says he doesn't even care about the homework-free week because first graders don't have much homework.

"I'm so happy everyone is so excited," says Joey.

I'm excited too. I feel like we're at the beginning of a race. We're ready. We're set. Now, off we go!

PROBLEMS AT THE START

"You can go in," Mr. Price says as soon as Joey and I walk into the office.

This is the second time this week Joey and I have been to see the principal. When we were here on Monday, I didn't think we'd be back so soon.

Mrs. Daily is already there with Mrs. Finney. "It seems we have a problem," says

Mrs. Finney as soon as we're seated.

Joey and I look at each other. That's pretty obvious. The reps for the food drive were chosen yesterday. Lots of kids signed up, which is a good thing.

Here's what's not so good. A lot of kids in fifth grade are upset Mary Ann and Zoe got picked to be the class reps. Since Mary Ann is Joey's stepsister and my friend, and Zoe is Mary Ann's friend, a lot of kids thought it was unfair, even though Mrs. Daily told everyone she did a random drawing to pick their names.

I was surprised Mary Ann even signed up to be a rep, since she said she wasn't interested when I asked her if she wanted to do the food drive with me. But she did, and now a bunch of people are mad.

Arielle said she thought the selection was rigged.

Danielle said that she and Arielle both wanted to be class reps and that they're going to boycott the food drive.

Half our grade isn't even speaking to Joey or me.

"I don't get why people are mad at us. Joey and I didn't have anything to do with who got picked to be reps," I say to Mrs. Finney and Mrs. Daily.

"That's true," says Mrs. Daily. "But we have the meeting with the reps this afternoon and we don't want to start the food drive with people feeling bad."

"We need to do a little damage control," says Mrs. Finney.

I'm not even sure what that means. I find out a little later that day. Mrs. Finney shows up at the music room while all the fifth graders are in class with Mom.

Everyone looks at me as the principal

motions Mom over to the door and talks to her. I don't usually mind that Mom is the music teacher, but today I do.

Mom at school = AWKWARD

It's bad enough that I'm part of the reason Mrs. Finney is here. It's even worse that Mom is involved too.

Mrs. Finney walks to the front of the music room and raises her hand to get everyone's attention. "I'm going to make this short and sweet," she says. Her voice sounds like she's conducting a business meeting.

"I'm counting on the fifth grade to be supportive of the food drive. Mary Ann Martin and Zoe Anderson are your class reps. They were chosen fairly, and I expect all of you to help them make this project a success."

Mrs. Finney pauses like she wants to be sure no one misses what she says next.

"I don't want to hear of one problem with this grade. In fact, I fully expect your grade to bring in the most cans and win that homework-free week. What do you say?"

Everyone cheers.

I guess that problem is solved. "Hopefully, we don't have any more problems this afternoon at the rep meeting," I whisper to Joey.

But the rep meeting doesn't go as smoothly as I'd hoped. First, Joey and I explain to the reps which canned goods the kids in their classes should bring in. "The Fern Falls Food Bank was very specific about what they want for Thanksgiving," says Joey.

"Just corn, green beans, sweet potatoes, pumpkin pie filling, gravy, and cranberry sauce," I tell the group.

"Did you say pumpkin pie filling and cranberry sauce?" asks Mike Parker, a third grader.

"Or did you say cranberry pie filling and pumpkin sauce?" asks Marcus Ling, the other third-grade rep. Both boys crack up, and some of the other kids laugh too.

I give Joey a *they're-being-wise-guys* look.

"What about peas and carrots? Those are good foods for Thanksgiving," says Lindsay Marshall, a first grader.

"So are onions," says her co-rep, Melissa Levy.

65

"Onions stink," says Amy Stark, one of the second-grade reps. She holds her nose like she doesn't even like thinking about the way onions smell.

The other second-grade rep, Tristan Williams, makes a retching noise.

There's more laughter. "Onions don't come in cans," says Annabelle Blake, one of the fourth-grade reps.

"Fried onions do," says Max Garcia, the other fourth-grade rep.

"How are we supposed to remember what's OK to bring in?" asks Jake Willensky, one of the sixth-grade reps.

Joey holds his hands up stop-sign style to get the others to stop talking. "We made a list of all the acceptable foods," he says.

Mrs. Daily hands me the copies we made of the list. "This will make it easy to share the information with your classes," she says.

As I start to pass them around, Zoe raises her hand. "Maybe we should make posters to show kids exactly what to bring."

"We could post them around school and in the classrooms," Mary Ann says like she's finishing Zoe's thought.

Mrs. Daily smiles. "That's an excellent idea." She sends Zoe and Mary Ann to her classroom to get poster board and markers.

I agree with Mrs. Daily that it's an excellent idea. I just wish Joey and I had thought of it.

When Mary Ann and Zoe return with the poster board, Mrs. Daily breaks the reps into small groups so there are younger kids

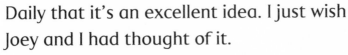

and older kids in each group. As the groups make posters, Joey and I explain how cans should be collected.

"It's a three-step process," I say. "Step one: tell the kids in your grade which foods to bring in. Step two: bring the cans you collect to the gym. Step three: put the cans in the area marked for your grade."

Joey shows the reps how we sectioned off and marked areas on one end of the gym for the reps to stack their cans.

"It's simple," I say. "When the food drive ends, we'll count the cans and the grade that brings in the most cans wins the homework-free week." When I'm done explaining, there are lots of questions. It's clear some of the reps don't think this is as simple as I do.

What if kids bring in the wrong kinds of cans?
What if kids bring in boxes instead of cans?

What if kids eat what they bring in?

As Mrs. Daily answers the questions, I can't help but think about an expression she taught us in third grade: *off to a rocky start.*

It means that a situation is difficult from the beginning.

When Joey and I talked to Mrs. Finney about doing the food drive, it seemed pretty simple. I never anticipated that kids in our class wouldn't be speaking to us or that the reps would have so many questions.

The food drive has definitely gotten off to a rocky start.

I just hope the rest of the voyage is smoother sailing.

KEEPING IT STRAIGHT

Last Friday, the reps talked to all the classes about the food drive. They put up the posters we made and told them which foods to bring in.

They reminded everyone that the grade that brings in the most cans wins the homework-free week.

It has been a week since the food drive

started. I expected kids to bring in lots of cans. But I never expected that this would turn into a problem.

Keeping the cans straight has been a big challenge. If you don't believe me, keep reading and you'll see what I mean.

MONDAY

Monday was the first day that kids could bring in cans. Joey and I were in the gym with Mrs. Daily during lunch when the second-grade reps, Tristan and Amy, brought in the bags of cans their grade had collected.

"Look how many cans we have," said Amy as they started taking cans out of the bags and stacking them in the second-grade area.

While they were stacking, Marcus and Mike brought in the bags of cans the third graders had collected. They put their bags down next to Amy and Tristan's and started stacking their cans in the third-grade area.

But while they were stacking, they got confused about whose bags were whose.

"That bag belongs to the second grade," said Tristan when Marcus picked up one of the bags and started taking cans out of it.

"It belongs to the third grade," said Marcus.

The next thing I knew, Tristan and Marcus were shouting over who brought the bag in.

Mrs. Daily stopped the argument. "That bag belongs to the second grade," she said as she took the bag from Marcus and handed it to Tristan.

All I can say is that I'm glad Mrs. Daily was there to be the referee.

TUESDAY

On Tuesday, there was another problem over who brought in which cans, but the problem didn't happen in the gym. It happened in the bathroom.

I didn't see the problem when it happened. But I heard about it.

Mary Ann told me she and Zoe stopped in the bathroom on their way to take the fifth grade's cans to the gym. When they went in, they had seven plastic grocery bags filled with cans, but when they came out, she said they only had six.

"While we were using the bathroom, we heard a group of sixth-grade girls come into the bathroom, and we think they took one of our bags," said Zoe.

Even though Mary Ann and Zoe seemed sure of what happened, I wasn't convinced. "If you were using the bathroom, how do you know it was sixth-grade girls who came into the bathroom?" I asked.

Inspector Mallory investigates the CASE of the MISSING CANS.

"By their shoes," said Mary Ann.

A lot of sixth-grade girls have cute shoes, so that made sense. But something else didn't. Why did Mary Ann and Zoe both have to go to the bathroom right then? Couldn't they have waited until after they'd dropped off the bags? Or taken turns so that one of them was always watching the bags? But I didn't say any of that, because I didn't want them to think I was blaming them.

Instead, I asked, "Is it possible you could have miscounted your bags?"

When I said that, Mary Ann and Zoe looked at each other.

"Don't you want the fifth grade to win the homework-free week?" asked Zoe.

"Whose side are you on?" Mary Ann asked me.

I told them that as head of the food drive, I'm on the side of fairness, but I don't think that was the side they wanted me to pick. It seemed like winning the homework-free week was more important to them than bringing in food for people who need it, which was the whole point of the food drive. The things they said bothered me for the rest of the day.

WEDNESDAY

On Wednesday, the problems over who brought in which cans continued. At lunch, all the reps from all the grades brought cans into the gym. By this point, there were a lot of cans, but the fourth grade had a lot more cans than any other grade.

Everyone noticed it. Especially one of the third-grade reps, Annabelle Blake. "What if people try to move cans so their grade will have more cans?" Annabelle asked.

Olivia Fine, one of the sixth-grade reps, rolled her eyes. "None of the reps are going to cheat," she said.

"For a homework-free week they might," said Annabelle.

Mrs. Daily spoke up. "I trust all the reps to be honest."

But Annabelle wasn't as trusting. "Maybe we need to hire a security guard to watch the cans," she said.

Mrs. Daily told Annabelle we're going to have to depend on an honor system and not a security guard.

THURSDAY

By Thursday, the cans were really stacking up. Every rep from every grade brought in more cans. Most of the cans were where they were supposed to be—in the sections for each grade. But some of the cans were in front of the sections and some of the cans were behind the sections. After school, Joey and I went to the gym with Mrs. Daily so we could straighten up the donations.

"It's kind of hard to tell which cans belong to which grade," said Joey.

"I think we should post a sign that reminds the reps to stack their cans neatly in the section for their grade," I said.

"That's a good idea," said Mrs. Daily. So Joey and I made a sign.

Then I made a wish that people would pay attention to it.

FRIDAY

Now it's Friday, and all day long, kids were still bringing in cans to school.

They were also talking about the food drive and how much they want to win the homework-free week.

I know this because Joey and I went to all the classrooms this morning to remind kids that Monday is the last day to bring in cans.

But no one needed reminding.

The first and second graders showed us the sticker charts their teachers had put up outside their classrooms.

"We get a sticker for every can we bring in," said one first grader.

"We want to get a lot of stickers," said a second grader.

"And we want to win the homework-free week," another second grader said. Then all the second graders started cheering.

When Joey and I went to visit the third
grade, they were rehearsing a song for the
Thanksgiving assembly next week. When
they finished singing, they told Joey and me
they'll be onstage twice at the assembly
next week.

"Once when we sing our song," said one
third grader.

"And a second time when we win the
homework-free week," said another third

grader. When he said that, the third graders all started clapping like that was exactly what they planned to do.

I was surprised how competitive the first, second, and third graders were. But they weren't competitive at all compared to the fourth, fifth, and sixth graders.

After school, reps from all the grades brought their cans to the gym and the fourth-, fifth-, and sixth-grade reps were all talking about how their grade was going to win the homework-free week.

"The fourth grade is just getting started," said Annabelle.

"The sixth grade is going to win," said Jake.

"You won't beat the fifth grade," said Zoe. "We're bringing in more cans on Monday."

I think Jake took that as a challenge because he said, "Game on." Then he gave Olivia a look like they needed to get their classmates to bring in more cans.

I felt like I needed to remind everyone what the food drive is really about. "Helping other people is what's important," I said.

"So is winning a homework-free week," said Jake.

When we left the gym, I told Joey I was excited everyone was so into the food drive, but I was also a little worried that maybe kids are *too* into winning the homework-free week.

"At least we're going to collect a lot of cans," he said.

Joey had a point. But still, I was worried that the hype over the homework-free week had gotten out of hand.

CANFUSION!

A riddle: What do you call a mix-up over cans?

Answer: CANfusion!

Get it? Unfortunately, there's nothing funny about the canfusion that is going on at Fern Falls Elementary.

The problems started this morning.

Today was the last day of the food drive. Kids from every grade—and not just the reps—brought cans to the gym. I think everyone was curious to see if they could tell which grade brought in the most cans.

By lunchtime, we realized we had a problem.

Joey, Mrs. Daily, and I went to the gym to try to straighten out the cans, but it was an impossible task. There were cans EVERYWHERE!

"What are we going to do?" I asked Mrs. Daily as I picked up a can of cranberry

sauce that was sitting in the middle of the gym floor.

She looked at all the cans like she was trying to figure it out. But before she had a chance to do that, Jake and Olivia and Zoe and Mary Ann came into the gym.

"Which grade brought in the most cans?" Jake asked.

They all looked curious, but it was pretty clear there wasn't a simple answer to Jake's question. "I'm afraid we have a mess on our hands," said Mrs. Daily. She picked up a can of green beans and a can of sweet potatoes that were sitting on the bleachers. "I don't see how we're going to be certain which grades brought in which cans."

That was definitely not the answer anyone wanted to hear.

"If you don't know which grade brought

in the most cans, how will you know which grade wins the homework-free week?" asked Mary Ann.

Mrs. Daily shook her head. "It doesn't seem that we will be able to know that."

Olivia gasped like what Mrs. Daily said was the worst thing she'd ever heard. Mary Ann, Zoe, and Jake all stood there open-mouthed with their arms crossed like they felt the same way.

"It's important to remember why we had a food drive," Mrs. Daily said.

But I had a feeling that the reps weren't listening to her.

Word spread faster than butter melting on pancakes that there was a mix-up over the cans. By the end of lunch, everyone knew about the problem.

"Is it true?" some second graders asked me.

"How did the cans get mixed up?" a
third grader asked Joey.

"We heard the contest is off," a group of
fourth graders said to us both.

Kids in every grade were talking about
how no one was going to win the contest.
Everyone was mad about it. To be more
specific, they were mad at Joey and me.

When the last bell rang, all I wanted to do was go home. But as I was leaving, Devon stopped me. "I'm sorry everyone is mad about the mix-up over the cans," he said. "I think it's great that we had a food drive, even if nobody wins the contest."

"Thanks," I said. I was glad somebody got it.

Devon had more to say, though. "I don't talk about this much," he told me. "But when I was little, my dad lost his job. Since there are five kids in my family, it was a pretty hard time for us. When we didn't have enough money and needed food, we went to a food bank and it really helped." He paused and looked at me.

I wasn't sure what to say. I hadn't realized his family had gone through such a tough time. "I'm really sorry that happened to your family," I told Devon.

"I just wanted you to know that what you're doing will make a lot of difference for a lot of people," he said.

I said I was really glad he told me the story.

All day, I had been worrying about the mix-up over the cans. But hearing Devon's story made the fact that everyone is mad at Joey and me seem less important. The homework-free week would be nice, but this food drive is really about doing something good in the community.

When I get to my street, I walk straight to the wish pond and sit on the bench by the edge of the pond.

I used to come here all the time when I wanted to make a wish. I haven't done it for a long time. I guess as I've gotten older, I've gotten more doubtful about the whole *make-a-wish-and-it-will-come-true* thing.

But right now, there's a wish I want to make.

Even though it seems kind of babyish, I pick up a stone on the side of the wish pond and squeeze my eyes shut.

I wish I can find a way to make sure that the whole school will remember why the food drive is important and that we can all focus on what really matters.

When I'm done making my wish, I throw my stone into the wish pond and I open my eyes. This is one wish that I sure hope comes true.

BAGGING IT

"Look on the bright side," says Mrs. Daily. "There are a lot of cans!"

That part is true. The food drive is over, and we definitely collected a lot of cans of corn, green beans, sweet potatoes, cranberry sauce, gravy, and pumpkin pie filling.

But as I look at the faces of the class reps who are packing those cans into bags for the food bank to pick up after the assembly tomorrow, no one looks very happy.

"I still can't believe the cans got mixed up," Max Garcia mumbles as we start to line up the bags of food along one side of the gym. "Everyone in my grade wanted to win the contest."

"The sixth grade wanted to win too," says Jake like he can sympathize with Max.

"So did the fifth grade," says Zoe.

"And the third grade," adds Marcus.

Before the first- and second-grade reps have a chance to say how much they wanted to win, Annabelle Blake joins in the conversation. "It was your job to keep the cans straight," she says to Joey and me.

Joey points to the sign we made. "It was *everyone's* job to keep the cans straight."

Mary Ann and Zoe roll their eyes like that doesn't change anything.

"No one gets the homework-free week like you promised," says Jake. "It's not fair."

"It's not just about a homework-free week," I say.

Mrs. Daily nods. "Mallory is right." She gestures to the bags that are now neatly stacked along one side of the gym. "Our efforts were more than successful," she says. "You all set out to help collect cans of food for people in need, and you should be very proud of the job that you did. This food will make a big difference to a lot of families in our community."

A bunch of the reps nod like they get it. But as we leave the gym to walk back to class, it's easy to see that everyone is still upset about the contest.

"I feel bad," says Joey.

"Me too," I say. "Even though the homework-free week wasn't the point of the food drive, I still feel like we let everyone down."

Joey nods. "I wish there was something we could do."

Suddenly an idea pops into my head. I don't know why I didn't think of it before. "Maybe there *is* something we can do," I say.

Even though no one is near us as we walk down the hallway, I lean over and whisper my idea into Joey's ear.

There's a good chance the person who needs to give the OK for my idea will *not* be OK with it.

Still, it can't hurt to try.

"What do you think?" I ask when I'm done explaining.

Joey looks at me and grins. "Let's give it a shot," he says.

As we walk down the hallway together, I can't help but think that this will be our third trip to the principal's office in the past two weeks.

Hopefully, it will be our last.

MAKING A DIFFERENCE

"Students, may I have your attention please?"

Mrs. Finney waits at the podium until everyone in the auditorium is quiet. "The food drive was a big success. We brought in a lot of food. These donations will go a long way to help people in our community who are in need. I'm so proud of everyone who participated, and I'd like you to give yourselves a big round of applause."

Mrs. Finney waits while the whole school claps. When the applause stops, she starts talking again.

"I know there was an unfortunate mix-up over the cans that were collected, which meant that it was impossible to know who won the homework-free week."

When she says that, some of the kids in the back of the auditorium boo.

I look at Joey, who is sitting in the chair next to me. Yesterday, Joey and I went to Mrs. Finney's office and explained the situation to her. Then I told her my idea for a solution. She said she would think about it, but she didn't promise anything.

I hold up my hands so Joey can see that my fingers on both hands are crossed. I really hope Mrs. Finney comes through.

She continues, "You all worked very hard, so I have made the decision that everyone at Fern Falls Elementary deserves to be a winner. When you return from Thanksgiving break, there will be no homework for anyone for a week."

When she says that, every student in the auditorium claps and cheers.

It takes a long time for everyone to settle down. Finally, Mrs. Finney clears her throat like she's not done talking. "It was

not my idea to do this. Mallory McDonald
and Joey Winston, who headed up the food
drive, suggested it. They thought this was
the only fair solution." She pauses and
smiles. "But I have to admit that I agree."

When she says that, there's a fresh
round of applause. Everyone who is sitting
near Joey and me high-fives us.

"I can't believe it!" says Grace.

"This is so cool," says Zoe.

"You're both geniuses!" Pete says to Joey and me.

Even Mary Ann tells us we did a great job. Everyone is talking about how amazing it is that the whole school will have no homework next week.

"I know you're all excited," says Mrs. Finney. "But we have a special guest with us who wants to talk to you. Students, I'd like to turn the program over to Mr. Lee, the director of the Fern Falls Food Bank."

A man joins Mrs. Finney onstage. She shakes his hand and steps back so he can stand at the podium. Mr. Lee smiles at the audience. "I wish I'd had a homework-free week when I went to school," he says.

Everyone laughs.

Then Mr. Lee gets a serious look on his face. "I want to thank all of you for participating in the food drive. Before the assembly, I went by the gym with Mrs. Finney and saw all of the bags of cans you collected. Because of your efforts, many families in Fern Falls will have a very special Thanksgiving."

He pauses and then continues. "What you have done has made a real difference in our community, and I want to thank you for all of your hard work."

He waits while everyone claps. "I also want to recognize a special teacher and some special students who helped lead the food drive." He calls Mrs. Daily onstage and thanks her for being the teacher in charge of the food drive.

Then he calls Joey, me, and all of the reps on to the stage with him. He presents a certificate to each of us.

Mrs. Daily takes a picture as we pose with Mr. Lee and our certificates.

When we're done, the third graders sing the Thanksgiving song they practiced.

Then Mrs. Finney wishes everyone a happy Thanksgiving and dismisses students to go back to their classes.

The reps follow Mrs. Daily to the gym to help take the bags of the food to the parking lot where the truck from the Fern Falls Food Bank is waiting. As I leave the gym, all my friends crowd around me.

"Mallory, you did an amazing job with the food drive," says Chloe Jennifer.

"You definitely did!" Pamela smiles at me like she's proud.

"It was a great idea," says April.

Even Arielle and Danielle have nice things to say.

"Now we want to do something that helps other people too," says Arielle.

"Maybe something for Christmas," adds Danielle.

"Thanks," I tell all my friends. As I head to the gym, I take a deep breath.

I'm really happy about the way things turned out. Fern Falls Elementary was able to do something good for the community. Everything worked out with the contest. I got a certificate of appreciation, and all my friends thought I did a good job.

It's almost Thanksgiving and I, Mallory McDonald, have a lot to put on the list of things I'm thankful for.

REASONS TO CHEER

The class reps carry the bags of food from the gym to the parking lot. But when we get there, there's more than just school buses and the food bank truck waiting for us.

There's also a news truck.

"Do you think we're going to be on TV?" I ask Joey as the crew gets out of their truck and starts setting up cameras.

Joey gives me an *I-have-no-idea-what's-going-on* look.

We watch as Mrs. Finney and Mr. Lee walk up to greet the news crew and another woman I don't recognize. Mrs. Finney shakes the woman's hand, and then she tells us she has two announcements to make. Everyone listens while she talks.

"Students, this is Mrs. Montgomery. She's the manager of Fern Falls Grocery. When I told her about your food drive, the store generously agreed to donate one hundred turkeys to go with all the canned goods you collected. That means one hundred families in Fern Falls will have everything they need for a complete Thanksgiving meal."

When she says that, all the reps cheer. That's great news—and it's so nice of the grocery store to be so generous.

But Mrs. Finney has more news. "What all of you have done to help families in need is pretty incredible, and I'm not the only one who thinks so."

She gestures to the news crew. "You're all going to be on the evening news!" When

she says that, all the reps burst out into more cheering.

Lindsay and Melissa start jumping up and down. "We're going to be famous!" shouts Lindsay. It's easy to see how excited she is.

Even though I'm too old to jump around and scream like a first grader, I'm pretty excited too. It's cool to think that what started as a small idea turned into something big.

"First, we want to film you kids loading the bags of the food onto the truck," says one of the camera crew from the TV station.

We all start picking up the bags and putting them on the truck. There are a lot more bags than there are reps. It takes a long time to load the truck.

As I'm carrying a bag to the truck, Mary Ann walks up beside me with a bag. "It's pretty cool that we're going to be on TV," she says.

"Yeah," I say. I can't help but think about the only other time we were on TV. It was when Mary Ann and I went to New York and were on the *Fashion Fran* show.

We were best friends when we did that, but a lot has changed since then. We used to do everything together. Lately, there have been a lot of things she hasn't wanted to do with me, including the food drive.

"I'm sorry I didn't want to plan the food

drive with you," Mary Ann says like she can read my mind.

"It's OK," I say. And it is. Even though

we're still friends, we're different. I get that we don't have to do everything together like we used to.

Mary Ann places her bag onto the truck and smiles at me. "You did a really good job. And I'm not just saying that because we got a homework-free week or because we're going to be on TV. It was a great idea, and it's cool that it's helping a lot of people."

"Thanks," I say, and I smile. It means a lot to me that she feels that way.

After we finish loading the bags, I stand back and look at the back of the truck. It's pretty impressive to see all the food that we collected.

I stand with the rest of the reps and watch as the reporter from the news station interviews Mrs. Finney and Mr. Lee and Mrs. Montgomery.

When they're done, I expect them to pack up their cameras and leave, but what happens next surprises me. "Mallory McDonald and Joey Winston," says the reporter.

Joey and I raise our hands, and the reporter motions us over to the spot in the parking lot where they were filming the interviews with the adults.

"As heads of the food drive, can you answer a few questions?" she asks.

"Sure," I say.

"I'm in," says Joey.

She motions to the cameras to start filming. "We're at Fern Falls Elementary with Mallory McDonald and Joey Winston, student heads of the food drive. What did organizing the effort mean to both of you?" She holds the microphone out to Joey like it's his turn to answer.

"I'm happy our school could help families have what they need for a Thanksgiving meal," says Joey.

The reporter moves the microphone to me.

"I'm happy we could help too," I say. "Even though we were the heads of the food drive, we couldn't have done it without our principal, Mrs. Finney; our adviser, Mrs. Daily; and all the students who brought in so many cans. It was a group effort."

"Thank you both." The reporter looks at the camera. "This is Nadia Gonzales reporting from Fern Falls Elementary." Nadia smiles at Joey and me. "Be sure to watch Channel 6 news tonight," she says. Then she motions to her camera crew to pack up their truck.

"Students, it's time to go back to your classes," announces Mrs. Finney.

But before we leave, Joey and I have something we both want to say to her. "Thanks again for everything you did to help us," Joey says. "Especially for giving everyone the homework-free week."

Mrs. Finney smiles at us. "I'm planning to make the food drive an annual event at Fern Falls Elementary," she says. Then she winks. "But next year, we're going to find a system to keep the cans organized."

I think that's the best idea I've heard all day!

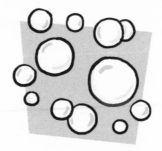

TV TIME

When I get home from school, I go straight to my bathroom. I turn on the hot water, pour in strawberry-scented bubble bath, and wait for the tub to fill with bubbles.

Once it does, I sink into the soapy water and think about the food drive. It was a lot of work, but I'm so glad I did it. Even though Joey and I just started it a few weeks ago, so much has happened since

then. Getting people to bring in cans,
keeping them organized, and then the
mix-up.

I'm just glad Mrs. Finney agreed to give
everyone a homework-free week. And I still
can't believe that the grocery store gave
away the turkeys or that the news crew
came to film it all.

When I finish my bath, I hop out of
the tub. As much as I love soaking in

bubbles, it's almost time for the Fern Falls nightly newscast.

I dry off and put on my coziest pajamas. I slip my feet into my fuzzy duck slippers and then I text Joey.

I skip to the den, where I plop down on the couch. I pick up the remote and turn on the TV. Mom, Dad, and Max join me. "I still can't believe I'm going to be interviewed on the news!" I say once they're all settled in.

Joey

News starts in 10 minutes

I'm already watching TV.

I don't want to miss it.

Neither do I.

We're going to be famous!

Ha-ha! Talk to you after it airs.

I wait for Max to roll his eyes like I'm making too big of a deal about this. But he doesn't. "It's pretty cool that you're going to be on TV," he says.

I smile at him. I'm excited about it. Being on the news isn't like eating breakfast or brushing your teeth. It's just not something that happens every day.

The first local news story is about an animal shelter that is having a special adoption day on Thanksgiving.

The next story is about a meeting at city hall. Then a story airs about how the Fern Falls Mall will open early and close late the day after Thanksgiving.

Even though the stories are interesting, what I want to see is the story about the food drive.

Luckily for me, it's the next story. "Here it is!" I yell. I'm so excited I can hardly sit still.

"That's Nadia!" I say as I point to the screen. "She was the reporter who interviewed Joey and me today."

We all listen as Nadia says she's
reporting from Fern Falls Elementary,
where students organized a food drive.
While she talks about the amount of
food that was collected, the report shows
students loading the truck from the Fern
Falls Food Bank.

"That's me!" I say.

By the time I get off the couch to point
to where I am on the screen, the report
cuts to Nadia interviewing Mr. Lee, Mrs.
Finney, and Mrs. Montgomery.

"I think the interview with Joey and me is
next," I tell my family.

But when their interview ends, so does
the report. The next thing that's on TV is a
commercial for laundry detergent.

"Hey, what happened to my interview?"
I ask.

Mom and Dad look at each other and

then at me. "Mallory, when a news crew covers a story, they film lots of things. But not everything they film ends up on air."

Mom stands up and puts her hand on my shoulder. "I'm sorry, Sweet Potato, but that sort of thing happens all the time."

She looks at me like she's waiting to see if I'm upset.

But I think my reaction surprises her.

"It's OK," I say. "I didn't do the food drive because I wanted to be interviewed on TV. It would have been cool. But I'm just glad I did something that helped other people."

I can tell my parents like hearing that.

"Mallory, we're so proud of everything you did," says Dad.

Mom wraps her arm around me and gives my shoulders a squeeze. "Because of you, a lot of people in Fern Falls are going to have a very nice holiday."

When she says that, I think about what happened to Devon and his family. Knowing that our food drive will help real people like him makes what I did feel even more important.

"And you got everyone at school a homework-free week," adds Max. "Nothing good like that happened when I went to school there."

I smile. I'm proud of myself for everything that I did. But it feels great to know that so many other people are proud of me—my teachers, my friends, my parents, and even my brother. "I'm really happy that the food drive went so well," I tell Mom, Dad, and Max. "I'm also happy that I got to do it with Joey. He's an amazing friend."

Right when I say that, I feel my phone

vibrate in my pocket. I check the screen and see that Joey's calling.

"Hey," I say when I answer.

"Hey," says Joey. "I guess we're not going to be famous."

I can't help but laugh. "Not yet anyway."

"Are you upset?" Joey asks.

Even though Joey can't see me, I shake my head. "Nope," I say. "No big deal. And there's always next year."

Now it's Joey's turn to laugh. "We just finished the food drive, and you're already thinking about doing it again next year?"

"Absolutely," I say. "Are you in?"

"For sure," says Joey.

"Good," I say. "Because I couldn't have done it without

you. Thanks for being an awesome partner."

"Yeah. You were too," he says.

We say good-bye and hang up. I feel all warm and fuzzy—and not because I'm wearing flannel pajamas or a warm robe or my fuzzy duck slippers. So many good things happened today.

I think back to how I felt on Halloween and how I feel now. It's hard to believe it all started because Dad read me that article about the high school kids who put on a Halloween party for underprivileged kids.

I remember how that girl, Jenny Perez, said it was the best Halloween ever.

Thanksgiving isn't until tomorrow, but I already know that it's going to be the best one I've ever had.

HAPPY
THANKSGIVING!

"Who wants turkey, and who wants ham?" asks Grandma.

"Can I have both?" asks Max.

Grandma laughs. "Why not?" she says. "It's Thanksgiving!"

Mom, Dad, Max, Grandma, and I all fill our plates with the feast that we spent the whole day making. Even though Mom

helped, and Max and I did too, Grandma
was the one in charge. She started cooking
as soon as she arrived this morning,
and the results are amazing. We have
ham, turkey, sweet potatoes, green
beans, stuffing, homemade rolls, and pie.
Everything looks delicious.

As I sit down to dinner with my family, I
can't help but think about the food that's on
my plate. Imagining what people's holidays
would be like if they didn't have enough food

makes me sad. I feel really good knowing I did something to help a lot of people who wouldn't have had enough to eat today.

"Honey Bee, you're awfully quiet," says Grandma.

I smile at her. She already knows about the food drive. It was the first thing I told her about when she got to our house this morning.

I told her about collecting the cans and the mix-up with the contest. I told her how Mrs. Finney ended up giving everyone a homework-free week and how the grocery store donated the turkeys and about the news crew that showed up. I even told her about my interview that never aired.

But what she doesn't know about is the poem I wrote last night before I went to sleep. I pull it out of my pocket. "I have something I want to read," I tell my family.

What I'm GRATEFUL for:
♡ By Mallory McDonald ♡

I'm grateful for the food on my plate.
I'm grateful for my parents.
You're both first rate.
I'm grateful for my brother.
You're never a bore.
I'm grateful for my cat (and dog)
that I LOVE and ADORE!
I'm grateful for my grandma,
who is so sweet.
Without you, my life would be incomplete.
I'm grateful for my friends.
They're fun and the best.
I'm grateful for my teachers.
They all pass the test!
I'm grateful for everything I have
(which is too much to list).
If I tried to name things,
there would be stuff that I missed.
Since today is Thanksgiving,
I just want to say
I'm grateful to be here on this special day.

When I finish reading, Grandma puts her fork down and claps. So do Mom, Dad, and even Max.

"Mallory, that was beautiful," says Grandma. "I'm glad to see that you're appreciative of all that you have. And I'm really proud of you for doing something to help other people in need. Just imagine if more people did things like that."

I smile. I know she's saying that if they did, the world would be a better place.

And I have to agree. But as I think about what she's saying, another thought pops into

Lend a hand.
Help the world.

my brain. And it's not one I'm proud of.

"Uh-oh," says Grandma. "A minute ago you were all smiles. Now why the frown?" she asks.

"I'm just thinking about how much better my Thanksgiving has been than my Halloween," I say.

Grandma is quiet like she's waiting for me to explain—so I do.

"On Halloween, I went to a party at Mary Ann's house, and then I tried to go trick-or-treating with Pamela and my other friends who didn't want to go to the party."

I eat a bite of turkey, and then I keep talking. "The only thing I was thinking about was what my friends were doing and what I was going to do. I didn't want to miss out on anything." I shrug. "It seems dumb now that I spent so much time worrying about it."

Mom passes around a basket of rolls.

"I think you're looking at it wrong," she says. "You saw that you didn't like how Halloween turned out, and you handled things differently for Thanksgiving."

That's true. I did. And I'm glad, even though there were some bumps along the way.

"You showed you're aware that the world is a big place—and that other people's lives and feelings matter as much as yours," says Grandma.

She opens her mouth like she's about to launch into a long speech, but Max stops her. He points to the pumpkin pie and the pecan pie on the counter. "Is it time for dessert yet?" he asks.

Grandma smiles at Max. "Almost," she says. "I just want to say one last thing while we're on the topic of making the world a better place."

Max looks at the pies on the counter. I can tell he hopes whatever Grandma has to say is quick.

"I won't be long-winded," Grandma says as she winks at Max. "In the holiday spirit, I just want to say that it is always better to give than it is to receive."

"I agree," I say.

Grandma smiles at me like she approves. "Now we're ready for pie," she says.

"Not so fast," says Max. "I have a question for Mallory."

Everyone looks at my brother as he looks at me. I think they're just as curious to hear Max's question as I am.

"You know Christmas is coming up soon," he says.

I nod. Everyone knows that.

Max grins. "So here's my question. On Christmas, would you rather give or receive?"

It doesn't take me long to think of my answer.

"Both!" I say.

A HOW-TO GUIDE

Being part of a community service project is a lot of fun, and it feels great to do something that helps other people. With a little bit of planning, a project can turn out even better than you imagined. I learned a lot when I organized the food drive.

Here's my ten-step guide to picking and putting together a great project.

Mallory McDonald's Ten-Step Guide to Planning a Great Community Service Project

STEP #1:

DETERMINE NEED. The first question to ask when planning a community service project is who or what do you want to help? There are so many groups that could use help—such as sick children, the elderly, homeless people, and abused animals.

STEP #2:

COME UP WITH A PLAN. Once you know what group you want to help, it's time to start planning. Talk to your parents, teachers, and community leaders to get ideas. Brainstorm, make lists, and decide on a project!

STEP #3:

GET OTHER PEOPLE INVOLVED. It's a lot more fun (and it works better too!) if you get other people involved in your project. Get your friends to volunteer. Ask your principal if you can post sign-up sheets or make an announcement at school.

STEP #4:

WORK AS A TEAM. When you're doing a project, you can't do everything yourself. Make sure everyone on your team has a job. If you all work together, you will get the job done.

STEP #5:

MAKE A SCHEDULE. It's important to make a schedule and stick to it, especially if there is a deadline to your project, like a holiday.

STEP #6:

SPREAD THE WORD. It's always a good idea to let other people know what you are doing. Talk to friends, family, businesses, and the news media. Pass out flyers. You never know who might want to volunteer or donate to your cause.

STEP #7:

LIGHTS, CAMERA, and ACTION! When it's time to put your plan into place, make sure you're ready. Check your to-do lists. Line up the supplies you need. Don't forget to bring a camera. You'll want pictures. Then it's time to get to work!

STEP #8:

CLEAN UP. Be sure to clean up when

your event or project is done.

STEP #9:

SAY THANK YOU. make a list of everyone who volunteered or donated and be sure to thank every person. You can write letters or e-mails, or  you can call people on the phone. People always like knowing they are appreciated.

STEP #10:

RELAX AND REFLECT. When your project is done, sit back and take the time to feel good knowing you've made a difference in your community. But also think about anything you could have done to make your project more successful. That way, you'll know what to do next time!

And if things go wrong, don't worry! There's a solution for every problem. I promise!

Good luck! I hope my tips help you plan an awesome community service project.

A SCRAPBOOK

I just counted, and I have twenty-three scrapbooks on my bookshelf. That sounds like a lot, and it is. Mary Ann and I made fourteen of them together, and I made the rest by myself.

I have scrapbooks from my trips to New York, the Grand Canyon, and Washington, DC. I have scrapbooks from holidays and birthdays. I even have one I made when we first moved to Wish Pond Road.

I love having them because when I look back at the special times in my life, the scrapbooks help me remember all the specific details.

It's a pretty cool way to keep track of all of those important events.

Of course, I made a scrapbook for this Thanksgiving too. How could I not? It was such a special holiday, and a lot of things happened that I feel so grateful for. My Thanksgiving scrapbook is packed full of pictures, but here are a few of my favorites.

Here's a picture of Joey and me organizing (or at least trying to!) the cans from the food drive. It was a lot of work, and of course, there were a few problems. But in the end, everything worked out great.

Here's a picture from the assembly when Mr. Lee gave the class reps our certificates.

I like it because you can see how surprised and excited everyone is.

Here's my certificate. I put it in my
scrapbook so I'll always know where it is.

Here's a picture of me with my family
on Thanksgiving Day. Don't Champ and
Cheeseburger look cute?

And last but not least, here's a picture
of me.

When Mom took this one of me on
Thanksgiving, she said she liked it
because I look very mature. She even
got kind of teary-eyed and said she

can't believe how old I'm getting and, even more importantly, how nicely I'm growing up.

"Do you mean how big and tall I'm getting?" I asked Mom.

Mom laughed and said that wasn't exactly what she meant.

"Are you talking about the kind of person I'm becoming?" I asked.

Mom nodded and gave me a hug. "Mallory, I'm so proud of you," she said. "You have exhibited real signs of maturity lately."

I didn't ask her what those signs were, but I kind of had an idea what she was talking about, and I have to admit, it made me proud of myself.

I had a great Thanksgiving, and not just because I was part of a project that helped so many people. I have an amazing family, great friends, an awesome cat, and everything I need—like a house, clothes, and food. I think what made Thanksgiving so special is that I realized how grateful I am for so many things in my life.

Is that a sign of maturity?

I, Mallory McDonald, think it just might be.

A Word from the Author

When I wrote the first Mallory book, I never dreamed that one day it would be a series with twenty-eight titles. But now it is, and there are so many people I would like to thank.

First and foremost, my kids, Adam and Becca Friedman. Growing up, you did so many things that provided inspiration for the books. Best of all, you were always great sports about having some of your most private moments revealed in print!

I'd also like to thank my mother, Annette Baim. Bless you for saving all those journals I kept when I was Mallory's age. It was the window I needed into my 3rd-, 4th-, and 5th- grade self.

My special and most sincere thanks to a group of people who have had a huge role in the development of this series. To my agent, Susan Cohen of PearlCo Literary, who has been by my side every step of the way. To all of the talented artists who have made Mallory look so good, especially Jennifer Kalis, who has drawn Mallory more times, more ways than I can count. And to the whole team at Lerner who has supported and worked on these books for years. Mallory would not exist without all of you.

And last but not least, my deepest thanks to my incredible editor, Amy Fitzgerald, who is an excellent character mama, and did a great job making sure Mallory grew up right.

From the bottom of my heart, thank you all.

L.B.F.

Darby Creek
A division of Lerner Publishing Group, Inc.
241 First Avenue North
Minneapolis, MN 55401 USA

For reading levels and more information, look up this title at
www.lernerbooks.com.

Cover background images: © iStockphoto.com/pshonka (turkey);
© iStockphoto.com/Lesya_Gnatiuk (cranberries); © iStockphoto.com/
johnnylemonseed (pies).

Main body text set in LumarcLL 14/20. Typeface provided by Linotype.

Library of Congress Cataloging-in-Publication Data

Names: Friedman, Laurie, 1964- author. | Kalis, Jennifer, illustrator.
Title: Mallory makes a difference / Laurie Friedman.
Description: Minneapolis : Darby Creek, [2017] | Series: Mallory ; #28
    | Summary: After having an awful Halloween, Mallory organizes a
    Thanksgiving food drive at her school, but it is harder than she expects
    and she has to consider whether she is doing it for the right reasons.
Identifiers: LCCN 2016023279 | ISBN 9781467750325 (lb : alk. paper)
Subjects: | CYAC: Food banks—Fiction. | Schools—Fiction. | Family life—Fiction.
    | Halloween—Fiction. | Thanksgiving Day—Fiction.
Classification: LCC PZ7.F89773 Mahe 2017 | DDC [Fic]—dc23

LC record available at https://lccn.loc.gov/2016023279

Manufactured in the United States of America
1-36608-17190-2/6/2017

SUSTAINABLE
FORESTRY
INITIATIVE

Certified Sourcing
www.sfiprogram.org
SFI-01268

SFI label applies to text stock only